George Junkin

The Two Commissions

the apostolical and the evangelical

George Junkin

The Two Commissions
the apostolical and the evangelical

ISBN/EAN: 9783337403744

Printed in Europe, USA, Canada, Australia, Japan

Cover: Foto ©Andreas Hilbeck / pixelio.de

More available books at **www.hansebooks.com**

THE TWO COMMISSIONS:

THE APOSTOLICAL

AND

THE EVANGELICAL.

BY GEORGE JUNKIN, D.D., LL.D.

PHILADELPHIA:

WILLIAM S. & ALFRED MARTIEN,

No. 606 CHESTNUT STREET.

1864.

CONTENTS.

CHAPTER I.

CHAPTER II.

CHAPTER III.

CHAPTER IV.

CHAPTER V.

CHAPTER VI.

CHAPTER VII.

CHAPTER VIII.

NOTICE AND DEDICATION.

THE following discussion, for substance, has been delivered on several occasions, as a sermon expository of the Gospel Commission. Having been kindly invited to participate in the installation services of a former pupil, the Rev. Robert M. Wallace, over the First Presbyterian Church of Altoona, Pa., the author repeated the discourse on that occasion, on the 6th of May, 1864. Whereupon, the clerical brethren present expressed a wish to have it put into a permanent form, as the views set forth were, in some respects, new to them. With this wish the present little book is a compliance, and a little more. As single sermons are generally unsaleable, and, indeed, seldom read beyond the narrow circle of personal friendship, it is deemed advisable to change the form entirely, to expand the substance considerably on some points, and to add several items to the "Practical Results." With these alterations, the little book is respectfully and affectionately dedicated to the Pastor and Church of Altoona, and the Brethren of the Presbytery of Huntingdon, by their friend,

THE AUTHOR.

Philadelphia, June, 1864.
1*

THE TWO COMMISSIONS.

CHAPTER I.

SOCIAL LAW AN ORIGINAL ELEMENT IN MAN'S NATURE.

GOD created man a social being; and that, both in regard to things natural and temporal; and in regard to things spiritual and eternal. *Society*, therefore, is an ordinance of God, by a direct creating act: and government, which is the agency established in society to manage its general interests, is a divine *Institution.* Many things, indeed, as to the minor details of business, both in civil and in religious society, so to speak, are left to human prudence and discretion: but the *principles* of law and order are all prescribed by divine authority. It is God's prerogative; and not man's, to create moral obligation. The laws of our intellectual, moral, and spiritual nature, are no more the product of human genius, than are the laws of mere physical nature. These last exist in the material world by the direct exercise of creating power. To search them out and avail ourselves of them, is our duty and our high privilege.

Newton's laws, Kepler's laws, are God's laws; existing in his works, before these distinguished philoso-
phers were born: the honor of discovery, not of
invention, is all that we can concede to human
genius. It only acquires the knowledge of methods
in the divine administration—the mode in which the
first cause acts. But even the more important of
these were not bodied forth at first only in the crea-
tion, and left for man to seek out by tedious and
slow processes of investigation. Man's ingenuity did
not discover the laws of vegetation, and then apply
them for the production of food and garden fruits:
God planted the garden, and taught him the use of
it: thus putting him in possession of the laws of
nature, and the modes of their application necessary
for his well being; and thus, by a practical government, forefending him against the destruction which
must have ensued, had he been left without a knowledge of these laws, until he discovered them by his
own researches and experiments.

So, neither did the Creator leave the intelligent
and social being, for a moment, without law and the
knowledge of it, but furnished him with a prophy-
lactic remedy against the destruction which anarchy
must have speedily produced. This remedy lies in
the fact, that moral law, and the subjects and exe-
cutive agents of it, were concreated. God did not
make man an intellectual and moral infant, and
leave him to feel his way, and discover, by plodding
search, the laws necessary to his continued social

existence and well-being. Then must he have perished; for the very first experiment might have been a sin; and if not the first, very soon must he have blundered upon some Fourierite or Mormon empirical scheme, in violation of the social laws of his nature, and lost all. The discovery of moral law, *a posteriori*, is impossible. The reason is, because the will of God made known as the rule of action is law: "My meat is to do the will of him that sent me." In the divine mind, so to speak, ere man became a living soul, the laws of his social nature existed, and were breathed into his nostrils along with the breath of life. And thus we avoid the absurd conception of an independent creature—a creature outside and beyond the range of its Creator's authority—a creature without law.

An agency there must be, for the transaction of business in and for the social body; and that, in respect both to its civil and its religious aspects: and this agency must have been originally and immediately appointed by the Creator himself. Now, what seems philosophically a necessity, does also appear to us historically a truth. Adam was divinely constituted, in both aspects, the head of his race. So, in the reconstruction of society under Noah: so, under Abraham: so, under Moses: so, under the divine Lord himself. In all these five cases, the incipient movements were all divine, supernatural, and miraculously attested. They are initiatory; introductory; or, as we now phrase it in regard to organizations of infinitely less importance, *provisional;* that is temporary, and leading forward to something stable and permanent.

Such seems also to be the law of our social nature, within the sphere allotted to human skill and prudence. Take, for illustration, a case of extreme simplicity—the formation of an association or society for the accomplishment of any right object—and none other can rightly be undertaken—say the establishment of a hospital. Some individual conceives and suggests to others the idea: notice is published, inviting persons like-minded to meet at such a time and place for this object: a crowd assembles—can they do anything without organization? without appointing officers? Or, will they not be a mere inert mass or a mob? What then is the obvious, simple, and usual method? Some person—most probably the original conceiver of the idea—assumes the responsibility—the prerogative, if you please—and nominates a temporary chairman, and calls the vote. Now we have a *provisional government.* The mass of individuals are no longer insulated and independent, but they constitute a body; one social body, organized and under law previously existing, for its own government; and as an organized body, with an object declaredly in view consistent with and promotive of the public good, it is under the protection of public law; no man may disturb it with impunity. This provisional government proceeds to a permanent organization for the accomplishment of their benevolent design: they adopt a constitution, appoint all necessary officers; and having exercised all proper powers of a provisional, merge themselves in the permanent government of the institution.

Now, from the innumerable instances of this kind, all over the face of society, are we not entitled, yea, constrained to infer, that the substance of such procedure is a necessity, and therefore a law of our social nature? And if so, must we not find it also within the sphere not only of morals, but also of religion? The *matter* in reference to which this law is brought to bear, changes not the law itself. Whether it be a hospital, a bank, a college, a railroad, or a church, the social law abides the same. Organization is necessary to the vital action of the social body; yea, to its very being as a body—*one body*. The Church must have officers in order to the action of its vital functions.

CHAPTER II.

THE CHURCH—A SOCIAL BODY UNDER THIS LAW— ORGANIZED UNDER THE ABRAHAMIC COVENANT.

IT is, perhaps, too obvious to require the remark here, that by *Church* we mean the Church *visible:* not the redeemed in heaven; not the elect; not true believers on earth; not regenerated and truly converted persons. These epithets designate the Church that is invisible; that is, they are not cognizable by our vision here in this world; they do not constitute a society—one society, which mortal eyes can here behold. But the Church of which we speak, is a visible body, consisting of all those who make a credible profession of the true religion—who call upon the name of our Lord Jesus Christ, together with their children. This visible Church includes most true believers on earth—the wheat of the parable—and often, alas! some tares—some whose whole religion is their profession; but none of those who have gone to glory; and none, as yet, who in an after period shall come out and be separate.

This visible Church, we hold, was organized under the covenant of God with Abraham, and not before. Prior to this, multitudes believed, and separated from the world; but, so far as we can read the record, were not organized under the dispensation of an external covenant, making its covenanters one body, known and recognized by outward visible signs and seals. But this point we may not discuss, because those who run farther back in search of the visible Church, do not dissent from our position, that it was organized under the Abrahamic covenant, and this is all that is necessary for our purpose. Two sacramental, outward, visible seals, are here recognized, sacrifice and circumcision, representing redemption by the death of Christ, the Lamb of God, and sanctification by the work of the Divine Spirit. This constitution, as it were, of the visible Church, had its government, its rules of admission and of exclusion. The start-point of its governmental administration was from God directly, and it was accompanied by supernatural and miraculous evidences. In Abraham was the provisional government, a sovereignty, a monarchy in fact. But the stock patriarchal shortly elaborated itself into a great number of aristocratic heads, until the days of Moses and Sinai.

The framework of this ecclesiastical constitution was most ample in its comprehension; it embraced the world; it made provision for the inbringing of the nations; it guaranteed that Abraham should be the heir of the world, the father of many nations; yea, that all nations should flow into it.

2

CHAPTER III.

THE SINAI COVENANT A RESTRICTIVE SYSTEM.

To this ecclesiastical constitution, under which the people professing godliness were organized into the visible Church, was superadded, four hundred and thirty years afterward, the restrictive enactments of Sinai. This did not abrogate the covenant, as Paul most abundantly demonstrates. In point of fact, the ceremonial regulations of Sinai are chiefly, if not entirely, evangelical institutions, having reference constantly to Messiah and the great salvation. By their misunderstanding and their perversion of them, the people, it is true, made them a yoke of bondage, just as unsound church members now do with church order and discipline; and their exclusive character, in the same way, made them repulsive to the heathen nations. This middle wall of partition was to remain in full strength as long as Israel proved faithful. Exod. xix. 5—8. "Now therefore, if ye will obey my voice indeed, and keep my covenant, then ye shall be a peculiar treasure unto me above all people: for all the earth is mine. And ye shall be unto me a kingdom of priests, and an holy nation. These are the words which thou shalt speak unto the children of Israel. And Moses came and called for the elders of the people, and laid before their faces all these words which the Lord commanded him. And all the people answered together, and said, All that the Lord hath spoken we will do. And Moses returned the words of the people unto the Lord." This covenant was renewed and expanded thirty-nine years afterward onthe borders of Canaan. You have the account in Deut. xxix. Very fully and distinctly does the Lord, by Moses, forewarn them of the fearful calamities that would follow their breach of this covenant of restriction, and of the glorious benefits of their faithfulness. So long as they stood in their integrity, they should be the Lord's peculiar treasure—a kingdom of priests; and so long, the gospel could not go forth on the broad basis of the Abrahamic covenant. But their unfaithfulness should open the door to the Gentiles, as Paul argues in Rom. xi. 11, "Through their fall salvation is come unto the Gentiles." Then, and not till then, could the gathering of the people be to Shiloh, the Peace-maker.

Here again we have the provisional administration. Moses stood between God and the people. He held the reins of government, and made considerable advances toward the separation of the civil from the ecclesiastical functions in the social body, ex. gr., in the institution of the priestly office and the Levitical consecration, and in the appointment of the grand, supreme court of the Sanhedrim, in the appointment of which he introduced the popular element. They were appointed by nomination and vote of the people, and thus a succession was secured.

The other element, important as a link in our chain of thought, is also fully supplied here. Miracles, very abundant, prove his divine mission, and give sanction to his legislation. The plagues and wonders in Egypt, the passage of the Red Sea, the perpetual miracle of the manna, the rock smitten, the garments not wearing out, &c., &c., all demonstrate the presence, power, and authority of the great and glorious God.

These Sinai restrictions upon the ecclesiastical constitution, glorious and terrible as was their introduction, and wise and benevolent as was the provisional government under which they were introduced, proved, as we have said, nevertheless a yoke of bondage and thraldom to that rebellious and stiff-necked people; yet they continued more than fifteen centuries. During this long stretch of ages, the doctrines of grace were illustrated and enforced, expounded and applied in almost infinite variety of methods, and by a vast diversity of agencies. One result of all that was spoken and written in the law of Moses, and in the Psalms and the Prophets, concerning the promised Seed of Abraham, was a high and glorious conception of his kingdom yet to come. His reign was expected, by all the faithful, to be a reign of peace, happiness, and prosperity; his dominion must extend from sea to sea, from the rising of the sun to the going down of the same, and all dominions shall serve and obey him. "His name shall endure for ever; his name shall be continued as long as the sun, and men shall be blessed in him; all nations shall call him blessed."

2*

CHAPTER IV.

THE KINGDOM OF MESSIAH: ITS PROVISIONAL GOV-
ERNMENT, THE APOSTOLICAL COMMISSION.

IN this kingdom of God—this blessed reign of
Christ—this administration which is not conducted
on the principles of this world, we shall find the
same category as in the Abrahamic and in the
Mosaic dispensations. That is, we shall find an
initiatory, a forming, a transition state—a *provisional*
government; and after this a full-formed and permanent state of things. The former is covered by
the Apostolical Commission; the latter by the Evangelical Commission.

The Apostolical Commission. Of this we have
three distinct records. Matt. x. 1—10. "And when
he had called unto him his twelve disciples, he gave
them power against unclean spirits, to cast them out,
and to heal all manner of sickness, and all manner of
disease. Now the names of the twelve apostles are
these; The first, Simon, who is called Peter, and
Andrew his brother; James the son of Zebedee, and
John his brother; Philip, and Bartholomew; Thomas,
and Matthew the publican; James the son of Al-
pheus, and Lebbeus, whose surname was Thaddeus;

Simon the Canaanite, and Judas Iscariot, who also betrayed him. These twelve Jesus sent forth, and commanded them, saying, Go not into the way of the Gentiles, and into any city of the Samaritans enter ye not. But go rather to the lost sheep of the house of Israel. And as ye go, preach, saying, The kingdom of heaven is at hand. Heal the sick, cleanse the lepers, raise the dead, cast out devils: freely ye have received, freely give. Provide neither gold, nor silver, nor brass in your purses; nor scrip for your journey, neither two coats, neither shoes, nor yet staves." And the entire chapter is taken up with a charge to them.

Mark iii. 13, 15. "And he goeth up into a mountain, and calleth unto him whom he would: and they came unto him. And he ordained twelve, that they should be with him, and that he might send them forth to preach, and to have power to heal sicknesses, and to cast out devils." Then follow the names, and nothing further.

Luke vi. 12, 13. "And it came to pass in those days, that he went out into a mountain to pray, and continued all night in prayer to God. And when it was day, he called unto him his disciples: and of them he chose twelve, whom also he named apostles." Then follows the list of names.

With these scriptures before us, let us link together the following remarks.

1. Christ himself did not live and minister under the New Testament dispensation, or kingdom of

God. Paul tells us, (Rom. xv. 8,) "that Jesus Christ was a minister of the circumcision." He closed his ministry before the kingdom was set up on the day of Pentecost: and he says himself, (Matt. xv. 24,) to the "woman of Canaan . . . I am not sent but unto the lost sheep of the house of Israel. . . . It is not meet to take the children's bread and to cast it to dogs."

2. The transcendent importance of the selection and ordination of the apostles, is manifested by the fact, that he spent the whole preceding night in prayer to God. I am aware, it is often said, he spent whole nights in prayer. It may have been so, but he has not so recorded it; that is the only instance of it.

3. This election and ordination occurred near the commencement of his own ministry in the Jewish church. The precise date cannot be ascertained; but these three records place it early. It could not have been long after the vocation of Peter and Andrew, of James and John.

4. The chief business of their ministry was to establish the fact of their Master's Messiahship; and to testify to his death and resurrection. This is manifest from several considerations. (1.) Their miraculous powers are set forward much more prominently than their preaching function. See Matt. x. 1—8; Mark iii. 15, and vi. 7—13; Luke ix. 1—6. So also the seventy (Luke x. 1—16,) to whom the same charge was given as to the twelve. In these

general instructions, the prohibition to provide supplies of money, food, and clothing, seems to refer to the miraculous supply of the church in the wilderness. (2.) But now, the well understood use of a miracle is to prove the divine mission of the person. Christ's own miracles, as Nicodemus alleges, had this effect, and those wrought by his missionaries, in his *name*—by his authority and power, that is—had the same design and force. (3.) To have seen Christ, both before his death and after his resurrection, was an indispensable qualification for the apostolate; this is manifest from the case of Matthias, Acts i. 20—22. "His bishopric let another take. Wherefore of these men which have companied with us, all the time that the Lord Jesus went in and out before us, beginning from the baptism of John, unto that same day that he was taken up from us, must one be ordained to be a witness with us of his resurrection." So, in the case of Paul, when his apostleship was questioned, he appealed to these facts, (1 Cor. ix. 1,) "Am I not an apostle? Am I not free? Have I not seen Jesus Christ our Lord?" Had he not seen Christ, both before and after his crucifixion, he could not have been "a witness with us of his resurrection." (4.) The preaching, which was of a very simple character, leads to the same point. "And as ye go, preach, saying, the kingdom of heaven is hand"—the time is near when the reign of the Messiah shall commence.

5. My fifth general remark is, that the apostolical

commission, as it was issued before his crucifixion, and whilst he was a minister of the circumcision, so it was, in express terms, limited as his own was, to the Jewish people—"the lost sheep of the house of Israel." Matt. x. 5, 6: "These twelve Jesus sent forth, and commanded them, saying, Go not into the way of the Gentiles, and into any city of the Samaritans enter ye not. But go rather to the lost sheep of the house of Israel." And so he said to the woman of Canaan, (Matt. xv. 24,) "I am not sent but to the lost sheep of the house of Israel."

Moreover, this express limitation has its counterpart in the actual fact, that they never went beyond the precincts of Judea, until after the new commission was given to them. And even when they went abroad, after they received the evangelical commission, the missionaries felt bound by the order, "beginning at Jerusalem," they always preached to the Jews first and only, (Acts xi. 19,) "preaching the word to none but to the Jews only." And it required the trance of Peter, (Acts x.) and the vision of the great sheet, to overcome this misconstruction of this new commission.

6. The reason is to be sought in the restriction by the Sinai covenant, which guaranteed religious privileges to the Jews, as the peculiar treasure and people of God. Until they proved unfaithful and broke their vows, the gathering of the nations to Shiloh could not take place. Christ could become the light of the Gentiles only after the seed of Abraham

should have put their light under a bushel. The evidences of their apostacy must be clear and indubitable, in order that, through their unbelief, salvation might go forth to the nations under the broad seal of the Abrahamic covenant. The natural branches must be cut off before the wild olive scions can be grafted in contrary to nature. "It was necessary," says Paul, (Acts xiii. 46,) "that the word of God should first have been spoken to you: but seeing ye put it from you, and judge yourselves unworthy of everlasting life, lo, we turn to the Gentiles."

7. One suggestion yet remains, viz., that no provision is made for the perpetuity, by transmission through human hands, of the apostolical commission. Apostles never were commanded, and never attempted to appoint apostles. On the contrary, Paul, who expressly admits an irregularity—at least a peculiarity in his own case—"as one born out of due time," very particularly and emphatically denies succession through human agency. Speaking to the Galatians (i. 12) of the gospel, he says, "I neither received it of man, neither was I taught it, but by revelation of Jesus Christ." And he proceeds to show that he was not called and ordained an apostle through any human instrumentality. No presbytery, nor synod, nor bench of bishops, had anything at all to do with his call and ordination to the apostleship. Verses 15—17, "But when it pleased God, who separated me from my mother's womb, and

called me by his grace, to reveal his Son in me, that I might preach him among the heathen; immediately I conferred not with flesh and blood: neither went I up to Jerusalem to them which were apostles before me." So great an event as the ordination of an apostle—and especially such a monster of wickedness as Saul had been—would undoubtedly have produced a sensation in Jerusalem. The very silence of Scripture on this point is no feeble proof that such an ordination never took place. But we have more than negative proof; for he declares, (Gal. i. 1,) "Paul, an apostle, (not of men, neither by man— [not *from* men—ἀπ' ἀνθρώπων; neither *through* man— δι' ἀνθρώπου,] but by [through] Jesus Christ and God the Father, who raised him from the dead.") Here he claims to be an apostle; he denies that he received the office through man's agency; he affirms that he received it directly from Jesus Christ; "by whom," as he says, (Rom. i. 5,) "we have received grace and apostleship." Accordingly, when he went up to Jerusalem, after his escape from Damascus, the apostles there refused to fellowship with him, until "Barnabas took him and brought him to the apostles, and declared unto them how he had seen the Lord in the way, and that he [the Lord] had spoken to him." (Acts ix. 27.) Demonstrably evident, then it is, that Paul was not ordained to the apostleship by and through man, but by Jesus in a personal interview.

The same is proved in the case of Matthias. The

bishopric of Judas was not conferred on Matthias by any college of bishops or of cardinals. They, indeed, cast lots, but they did it as an appeal to God; for they knew that "the lot is cast into the lap: but the whole disposing thereof is of the Lord." (Prov. xvi. 33)—more literally, its judgment from Jehovah. These men, knowing that none but our Lord personally could appoint an apostle, prayed and said, "Thou, Lord, which knowest the hearts of all men, show us whether of these two thou hast chosen, that he may take part of this ministry and apostleship, from which Judas by transgression fell." (Acts i. 24, 25.) They assume it, that their Lord only could make an apostle, and that he had chosen the man; and there being two, and but two, who had all the indispensable prerequisites, viz., companying with them, seeing Jesus before and after his death, they thus ask him to point out which he had chosen. Matthias was made an apostle, not by man, but by the Lord and King.

Thus, as in all former cases, we have a preliminary and temporary arrangement—a *provisional* government—in many things analogous to our national affairs, from the Declaration to the full organization under the Constitution. The apostolical office, attended by high and strong powers, and miraculous gifts, fills up the gap between the Mosaic and the evangelical dispensation. Our next topic will give us less trouble.

3

CHAPTER V.

THE EVANGELICAL COMMISSION.

THE record, Matt. xxviii. 18—20, "And Jesus came and spake unto them, saying, All power is given unto me in heaven and in earth. Go ye therefore, and teach all nations, baptizing them in the name of the Father, and of the Son, and of the Holy Ghost: teaching them to observe all things whatsoever I have commanded you: and lo, I am with you always, even unto the end of the world. Amen."

Mark xvi. 15, "Go ye into all the world, and preach the gospel to every creature. He that believeth, and is baptized, shall be saved; but he that believeth not, shall be damned."

The other evangelists record not the express language of the commission, but many of the remarks and instructions uttered in connection with it; and especially "that repentance and remission of sins should be preached in his name among all nations, beginning at Jerusalem;" and directing them to "tarry in the city of Jerusalem, until ye be endued with power from on high;" that is, until the day of Pentecost, when the kingdom proper should be set up.

1. On this we remark: The date of this commission was after our Lord's resurrection, and immediately before his ascension, and, of course about three years after the preliminary commission. This, as a link in our chain of thought, is all-important; but so evident and undeniable, as to render delay for proof and illustration entirely unnecessary.

2. It is based on this ground, that all power is given to him. And several subordinate observations will be proper. (1.) The power or authority is *given* to him. As God, it is obvious, no power could be *given*, for "all things were made by him, and without him was not any thing made, that was made," (John i. 3.) But as Mediator, as God-man, authority is derived, conferred, bestowed upon him; it is an *acquisition*.

(2.) This giving universal authority to the Mediator, is the reward of his work. He has finished the work which his Father had, in the councils of eternity, assigned to him, and which he had voluntarily assumed; he had paid the full ransom price, and fulfilled all righteousness; consequently he must receive his reward, and the means of vindicating the rights of his purchase. A right by purchase, involves the ability to vindicate, possess, and occupy. The giving of all power to Christ is, therefore, not to him a *gratuity*, but the concession of his *right* to rule the universe.

(3.) Prior to the concession and possession of this right, Jesus had no authority to send his ambassadors beyond the limits of the Sinai covenant. But now, having the heathen for his inheritance by appointment of the Father, through his own fulfilment of all the terms of the covenant, his is the earth and the fulness thereof. Having broken down the middle wall of partition, he has a right to command the nations all to enter in through the rent vail of his own flesh. Here is the foundation, true, and real, and just—the Rock, whence flow the living waters all over this desert world. Therefore my

3d. General remark. Note the amplitude of range which this commission takes. "And the kingdom and dominion, and the greatness of the kingdom under the whole heaven, shall be given to the people of the saints of the Most High, whose kingdom is an everlasting kingdom, and all dominions shall serve and obey him." (Dan. vii. 27.)

4. The function most prominent in this great commission, is the communication of sacred truth to the minds of men. One record says, "Go, teach;" the other, "Go, preach the gospel;" the matter of the instruction unites the two statements: "All things whatsoever I have commanded you."

5. The administration of the sacraments is embraced. Baptism is expressly mentioned, and the sacred supper is one of the most prominent things commanded to be observed. "This do in remembrance of me." The same is true of the administration of discipline in the Church. Many orders have

been given to withdraw from disorderly persons; to exclude them from the Church.

6. The *promise*, "Lo I am with you, &c.," may be considered as involving three things. (1.) The persons to whom it is addressed. And negatively we note, it is not addressed to apostles as such. Every one of the gospel historians ignores that term in this connection, except that the women use it once. (Luke xxiv. 10.) In no instance are the recipients of this commission called *apostles*. But, positively, it is addressed to "the disciples,"—"the eleven disciples,"—"the eleven." In the entire post-resurrection history by the four evangelists, the word *disciple* is used eight times, (only by John in application to himself); the plural, *disciples*, is used nineteen times, and often when the term *apostles* would seem most convenient and precise. For what reason? unless to preclude the idea that the commission was given to them as apostles in the technical or official sense.

The recipients of this commission, no doubt, include the eleven who had been ordained apostles; but the commission itself, with the appended promise, is different, and others were comprehended under the term disciples. When Matthias was appointed by the Lord, Peter's speech (Acts i. 15—22) seems to have been the only one made. "And in those days Peter stood up in the midst of the disciples, and said, (the number of the names together were about an hundred and twenty,) Men and brethren, this Scripture must needs have been ful-

3*

filled, &c." Indisputably, he addressed the hundred and twenty disciples, and not the eleven apostles only; and to the *disciples* as such, and not to the *apostles* as such, was the evangelical commission also given. Cases like this are of perpetual occurrence all over the face of society; office is often added to office, and generally in an ascending series. The ambassador to Portugal becomes Minister Plenipotentiary to France or to England, but by a new commission. The Secretary of Legation, anon, becomes Minister; the colonel is soon a general; the deacon of last year is an elder to-day, and next year the same man is a minister; Stephen is commissioned "to serve tables;" again he receives another commission, and becomes a public preacher of the word.

(2.) The matter of the promise is not specifically detailed, but obviously implied. To be constantly along with a person appointed and called to the performance of arduous duties, is a pledge of all needed aid; and without this promise few would consent, and none properly qualified would agree to go.

(3.) The perpetuity of this commission is here affirmed. Christ pledges his constant presence "unto the end of the world." As it has no limit in space short of the whole world, so it has no limit in time, but where time confines on eternity. Here then is the doctrine of succession. As a score or two of years must soon earth up all the disciples to whom directly the commission is given, it is obvious that the perpetuity of the Master's divine presence with his teachers, even to the end of the world, is impossible on any other supposition, but that of a regular succession of officers; and the subsequent history assures us they so understood their commission, for everywhere they ordained elders, evangelists, and pastors.

CHAPTER VI.

THE TWO COMMISSIONS COMPARED—CONTRASTED.

1. THEY agree in their divine origin. Both are from God, and are comprehended and ensured by the covenant of grace, before the world was made, and therefore display his everlasting love, and boundless mercy. Consequently,

2. They agree as to the substantial matter of their teaching. Salvation by grace, through the obedience, sufferings, and death of the woman's seed, the seed of Abraham—the root and the offspring of David—is the grand substance of both. The gospel is preached unto us, as well as unto them.

3. They agree as to the general character of the agencies they create. These are ambassadors—persons sent by due authority, and clothed with functions which they are bound to execute, according to the orders of Him that sent them. Both classes are *missionaries.* This last word is Latin, and a correct translation of the Greek word *apostles;* meaning, simply, *persons sent.*

POINTS OF DIFFERENCE.

1. They differ as to date. The Apostolical Commission was issued to the whole twelve at once, and at the beginning of Christ's public ministry; when, to use a political nomenclature, he formed his Cabinet. The Evangelical Commission was uttered after he had finished up all else of his work and sufferings on earth, and arisen from the dead; and was just about to ascend, to possess his throne in the heavens.

2. They differ as to the basis of authority. The Apostolic Commission, though having its remote foundation in the covenant with Abraham, yet is it modified by the restrictive covenant at Sinai. The Evangelical Commission has its foundation on the broad basis of Abraham's covenant, in rescuing which from the Sinai restrictions, by his obedience, death, and resurrection, our Saviour has vindicated to himself all power in heaven and in earth; and here has laid down its enduring foundation: "Go ye, therefore, and disciple all nations."

3. As a consequence, they differ as to extent of range in *space*. The Apostolic was limited to the lost sheep of the house of Israel; the Evangelical embraces all nations. The Star of Bethlehem glimmered over the narrow field of Judea, and then set in blood on Calvary; the Sun of Righteousness rises from the mortal bondage of the rocky tomb, and bursts over all the earth.

4. The Commissions differ in *time*. The one terminates with the fading life of the immediate recipients, there being no provision in it for succession; the other has the Divine guarantee that it shall endure to the end of the world. Of it the evangelical prophet speaks, (Isa. lxii.) "The Gentiles shall see thy righteousness, and all kings thy glory." And it is of this commission he speaks, (ver. 6:) "I have set watchmen upon thy walls, O Jerusalem, which shall never hold their peace, day nor night."

5. They differ as to their outward, visible ordinances. The one is concerned with Jewish lustrations—the passover, and divers other ceremonial sacrifices, looking forward to a Messiah yet to come, and offer up the great sacrifice; the other, with the sacred supper, looking backward to a finished atonement, by the perfected sacrifice of the Lamb of God, and a baptism of water and of the Holy Ghost, in the name of the ever blessed Trinity.

6. They differ as to the prominence of miracles. The Apostolic, designed to prove Christ's Messiahship, looks ever to miraculous works for its main efficiency; the Evangelical, though aided by miracles, relies mainly on the word of truth, brought home by the Spirit, for conviction, conversion, and sanctification.

7. Lastly, they differ in this, that the Apostolical Commission is part and portion of a transition—reforming state of the Church—a *provisional* government, in fact; the winding up of a dispensation,

indeed, of long but limited duration; a kingdom that can be moved, for the purpose of preparing for one that cannot be moved. (Heb. xii. 28.) The Evangelical Commission opens up a new economy; inaugurates an administration, permanent, glorious, and everlasting as the throne whence it emanates.

CHAPTER VII.

OBJECTIONS—1. THE NAME, APOSTLE, CONTINUES.
2. THE FUNCTIONS CONTINUE. 3. PAUL WAS AN
APOSTLE.

THE objection arises very naturally—"But the name, *apostle*, continues to be used as an official term, notwithstanding the issuance of the Evangelical Commission: this proves that the office is not abolished; that the alleged new commission is really only an enlargement of the powers of the old."

To these the answers are as obvious as the objections are natural.

(1.) The term *apostle* is sometimes used in its generic meaning as a noun common. So it is applied to the Saviour himself, (Heb. iii. 1:) "Consider the Apostle and High Priest of our profession, Christ Jesus." So, Paul's kinsmen (Rom. xvi. 7,) Andronicus and Junia, being of note among the apostles, surely does not mean, that they were apostles in the official, technical sense; but simply, that they were noted in the mission at Corinth. And in 2 Cor. viii. 23, Paul surely does not mean, when he speaks of "our brethren—as the apostles of the churches"—to affirm these messengers, as we translate the word *apostles*, to be such in the official and technical sense; nor that Epaphroditus was an apostle, (Phil. ii. 25.)

(2.) Terms of office very frequently continue after the functions, and even the office itself has expired. We 'have captains, and colonels, and generals, by hundreds, who are out of office, and have no company, or regiment, or brigade to command. We have sheriffs, and judges, and governors out of office, yet still so designated. We have ministers that do not preach, and doctors of divinity that do not teach theology.

(3.) But our main response is, that the inference is illogical. For, whilst we admit the fact, that the Apostolical office and name continue, we hold to it as a part of our doctrine, and it cannot be made to bear against us. We have never taught or believed that the Apostolic Commission was at any time withdrawn, or that any of its functions were recalled; and, consequently, do not hold that the name, *Apostle*, in its strict, technical, official meaning, does not frequently occur in New Testament use, since the issuing of the Evangelical Commission. On the contrary, we maintain that the office and the Commission Apostolic continues; but only in the hands of those individual men who received it from Christ. With them it lived; with them it died out. Moreover, they—perhaps all, but certainly most of them— received, along with others, a new, enlarged, and more glorious commission, whose functions never

4

die out with the death of the individuals, but endure "even to the end of the world."

As to the allegation that the evangelical is not a new, but only an enlargement of the apostolical commission, by the superaddition of some new powers, we suppose the last chapter has shut the door against it, and we need not add another word.

An objection is brought against our doctrine, with great plausibility, from the case of Paul. It is asked in triumph, What do you say to the Apostle to the Gentiles? Does not the very designation upset your whole theory? Did not Paul say, "Lo, we turn to the Gentiles"? (Acts xiii. 46;) and (Acts xxii. 21) does not the Lord tell him, "For I will send thee far hence to the Gentiles"? And Paul himself tells the Romans (xv. 15, 16) that, "Nevertheless, brethren, I have written the more boldly unto you in some sort, as putting you in mind, because of the grace that is given to me of God; That I should be the minister of Jesus Christ to the Gentiles, ministering the gospel of God, that the offering up of the Gentiles might be acceptable, being sanctified by the Holy Ghost." This is the objection.

As to the fact of Paul's apostleship, there is no dispute; and as little room is there for any question about his preaching to the Gentiles. Other apostles, probably all of them, did the same. But in regard to the original apostles, we have seen, at some length, that they received a new and more extended and glorious commission, and that under this it was that they preached to the heathen. But again, it is objected that, in 1 Cor. ix. 2, Paul seems to affirm his apostleship to have a special reference to them. "If I be not an apostle unto others, yet doubtless I am to you: for the seal of mine apostleship are ye in the Lord."

To this as an objection, we answer, (1) that the Greek word, both in its verbal and nominal form, is, as before stated, used in its generic sense; and thus is the noun to be understood in this passage—a *missionary*. "If I be not a missionary of God to others, doubtless I am to you, for your conversion to God is the seal of my mission." So would I read Rom. i. 5, "By whom we have received grace and a mission."

But (2) and chiefly, Paul, whilst he admitted an irregularity in his call and appointment, as "one born out of due time," and asserts that, "last of all, Christ was seen of him"—an indispensable condition for the apostleship—and whilst he labored more abundantly than they all, (1 Cor. xv. 7—10,) yet did he not go to the Gentiles under his apostolical commission. This he was called to on his way to Damascus, (Acts ix. 19, 20.) "Then was Saul certain days with the disciples at Damascus. And straightway he preached Christ in the synagogues, that he is the Son of God"—this being the burden of his commission. He dealt only with the Jews— v. 22—"confounding the Jews which dwelt at

Damascus, proving that this is very Christ. And after that many days were fulfilled, the Jews took counsel to kill him." "At Jerusalem also he preached the same, and disputed boldly against the Grecians," (v. 29)—not heathen, but Jews from Greece. "But they went about to slay him. Which when the brethren knew, they brought him down to Cesarea, and sent him forth to Tarsus." This, however, was probably on his second, if not his third, visit to Jerusalem; for he tells us (Galat. i. 17, 18) that "Neither went I up to Jerusalem to them which were apostles before me; but I went into Arabia, and returned again unto Damascus. Then, after three years, I went up to Jerusalem to see Peter, and abode with him fifteen days. . . . Afterwards I came into the regions of Syria and Cilicia." (Gal. ii. 1,) "Then, fourteen years after, I went up again to Jerusalem with Barnabas, and took Titus with me also." This is the visit mentioned in Acts xi. 30, when the disciples sent relief to the brethren at Jerusalem, "by the hands of Barnabas and Saul," who returned to Antioch when they had fulfilled their ministry. (Acts xii. 25.) During all these movements, the disciples "travelled as far as Phenice, and Cyprus, and Antioch, preaching the word to none but to the Jews only." (Acts xi. 19.) But after Peter's vision of the great sheet, and after the decision of the brethren at Jerusalem on that subject, "they glorified God, saying, Then hath God also to the Gentiles granted repentance unto life."

(Acts xi. 18.) Then followed a glorious revival at Antioch, and "tidings of these things came unto the ears of the church which was in Jerusalem, and they sent forth Barnabas, that he should go as far as Antioch;" and he labored with great zeal and efficiency, "and much people was added unto the Lord. Then departed Barnabas to Tarsus, for to seek Saul: And when he had found him, he brought him unto Antioch: And it came to pass, that a whole year they assembled themselves with the church, and taught much people." (Acts xi. 25, 26.) But whilst this revival was progressing among "the Jews only," and "the Grecians," "the Holy Ghost said, Separate me Barnabas and Saul, for the work whereunto I have called them. And when they had fasted and prayed, and laid their hands on them, they sent them away." They released (ἀπέλυσαν) them from their charge. Here we have the record of the ordination of Paul by the Presbytery of Antioch. To this high honor he refers in Eph. iii. 8, "That I should preach among the Gentiles the unsearchable riches of Christ." And 1 Tim. ii. 7, "I am ordained . . . a teacher of the Gentiles;" and 2 Timothy i. 11, "I am appointed a preacher, and an apostle, and a teacher of the Gentiles;" and Gal. ii. 9, "They gave to me and Barnabas the right hands of fellowship, that we should go unto the heathen."

Now a great door and effectual is open before him. He has received the Evangelical Commission through

4*

the hands of men, whereas he declares his Apostolical Commission was not received by men, or through men's agency, but directly and immediately from Christ himself. He is now a missionary, an evangelist to the Gentiles. Now is fulfilled the Divine purpose, announced to Ananias, (Acts ix. 15,) that "Saul is a chosen vessel unto me, to bear my name before the Gentiles, and kings, and the children of Israel;" the commission is conferred in the usual method of ordination, by fasting and prayer, and "the laying on of the hands of the Presbytery." (See 1 Tim. iv. 14.) In this case, it appears, the revival had attracted many to Antioch, and, observing the efficiency of Paul's services. they proceeded to his ordination. There were present, besides Barnabas and Saul, "Simeon, that was called Niger, and Lucius of Cyrene, and Manaen," (Acts xiii. 1); and also, as Paul tells us, (Gal. ii. 9,) "James, Cephas, and John," who seemed to be pillars, united and "gave the right hand of fellowship." Prior to this he had no authority to go beyond the lost sheep of the house of Israel, to whom his first commission, miraculously conferred, was limited. There is no evidence that he or any other apostle, as an apostle, ever preached to the heathen. The Evangelical Commission must supervene.

CHAPTER VIII.

PRACTICAL RESULTS.

1. THERE is an authorized ministry in the church; and an orderly method provided for its perpetuation. "No man taketh this honor unto himself, but he that is called of God, as was Aaron." This divine vocation is first inward by the Spirit; then outward, by the providences of God opening the way and furnishing the proper qualifications; and then outward also, by the vocation of the people of God—the disciples must be heard. The voice of the Lord, speaking by his Holy Spirit in the hearts of his own people, is an essential part of the heavenly call. This element secures religious liberty in the church. Let ministers make ministers *ad libitem*, and the people of the Church are saddled with a despotic power, that, in the end, crushes out both liberty and religion.

2. A system, therefore, of probation, is of incalculable importance. "Lay hands suddenly on no man;" let no man be hastily thrust into the sacred office, as either teacher or ruler; and even the deacons, who are appointed to serve tables, "must first

be proved." It has often appeared to me, that the very salutary regulations laid down in our Constitution are too little regarded. Young men are hurried away from our Seminaries; extra Presbyteries are often called to ordain them, before they have been tried and proved by a hearing before the disciples and churches. The public voice of the godly is never heard; they have the private recommendation of a Professor, but there is no opportunity for the people to "perceive the grace that was given to them." A few sermons, on which they have spent a large portion of their seminary labors, fill their side pockets, and pass off very well; but when these polished shafts are all drawn from the quiver, a change overshadows the pulpit; the light grows dim, the audiences diminish; a bad cold, a bronchial affection, calls upon the Presbytery to dissolve the pastoral relation; a string of deeply regretting resolutions accompany the painful acquiescence for its necessity; and the call, which, may chance, never was the intelligent voice of the pious people of the congregation, is returned to the Presbytery; and so they wrap it up. Such are some of the painful consequences of our departure from the old landmarks of our Book. Why, dear reader, it has become very extensively a custom with Presbyteries, to assign trial pieces for licensure, when a young man is first taken under their care as a candidate, and before he has begun the study of theology! Can we expect the Lord to protect the Church from the dreadful evil of so many without charges, while we neglect our own salutary rules?

3. Foreign missionaries ought not to be boys, just from the schools of the prophets. The legions of error and death are not to be overwhelmed by a squad of "recumbent virtue's downy doctors." If Vicksburg is to be carried, you must send a Grant; if New Orleans, you must send a Farragut and a Butler: if Gettysburg, you must send a Meade, a Howard, a Sedgwick. If Rome is to be reduced to the feet of Jesus, you must send a Peter; if Antioch, a Barnabas; if Ephesus, Corinth, and proud Athens, you must send a Paul. These observations are not retrospective. We have and have had a very fair proportion of the right kind of men in the foreign field. Let us continue this policy and a little more.

4. The Evangelical Commission is superior, greatly superior in dignity, excellence, glory, and duration, to the Apostolical, with all its extraordinary and supernatural powers. The scaffolding, the shears, and other machinery, are greatly inferior to the building which they have assisted to construct. When their purpose is subserved, they are removed, that the permanent structure may stand forth in all its beauty, that the nations may shout, Grace! Grace unto it. So thought Paul, when he devoted himself to the life of an itinerant missionary. So, in mercy to the Church over all the earth, may Barnabases and Pauls be enabled and constrained to think, until Zion shall arise and shine, because her light is come.

5. Claimants to apostolical succession have no authority to preach, "but to the Jews only"—"to the lost sheep of the house of Israel." "Go not in the way of the Gentiles."

6. The great duty of the Christian ministry is, to teach the things of Christ—to "teach all nations to observe all things whatsoever I have commanded you." Bible exposition is the soul of pulpit labor. But here it is proper to remark, that the contents of the sacred volume are vastly various, and not at all equally important. No topic can well enter the mind of mortal man, which may not be found less or more distinctly mentioned in the Book. Geogeny, geology, mineralogy, botany, zoölogy, astronomy, and a hundred other sciences, can find a text to present them. Mental and moral science, anthropology, and theology; history, natural, profane, and sacred; all possible subjects may be found. Obviously, however, those that lie at the foundation of a sinner's hopes for eternity, are those which must occupy the bearer of the Evangelical Commission, for the gospel is a remedial law. Bible exposition, however, there is reason to fear, is not the characteristic of pulpit services in our land. Scarcely any minister conducts a continuous exposition of any book of Scripture in the pulpit. The public taste will rarely tolerate it. The press has supplanted the pulpit, both in this regard, and in regard to quantity of preaching, as measured by time. Public taste can tolerate two, three, or four

hours of speech-making on politics, science, slavery, or war; but an hour's discourse on the issues of eternity and the judgment-day would be utterly unbearable. Is this owing to the vastly increased power of analysis in the pulpit, or of synthesis in the pews? It may be, but I doubt it.

7. The administration of the sacraments is another function of this office, but of a lower order. Both sacraments set forth fundamental doctrine; and these, in connection with discipline in the Church, which belongs largely to the ruling elders, are very importantly concerned in the preservation of her purity; and without purity, her power for good soon vanishes away. Of course, old women's or young nurses' baptism is not an ordinance coming under the functions of this commission; neither do masses, charged and paid for at five shillings apiece, have any efficacy in evangelizing the world, and saving men from death, the grave, and eternal torments.

8. How fearful, then, in view of this grand and glorious Commission, are the responsibilities of the Church! A lost world hangs upon the faithful discharge of its duties. Oh, let us hearken to the startling inquiry, "Whom shall I send? and who will go for us?" Oh, young men of America, by hundreds of thousands you have heard the call of your country, and have sprung forward to her relief. You have done well. But when this, your terrible service, shall have been finished up, there will present itself a field far more extensive; battles

of the warrior far more interesting and glorious
than those which are with confused noise, and garments rolled in blood. Over this revolted world
your Lord claims rightfully a right of absolute
dominion. He is marshalling his forces for the
battle and for the victory. Already rides he forth
upon his white horse. Faithful and True is He; in
righteousness doth he judge and make war; his
eyes are as a flame of fire, and on his head are many
crowns; and his name is called, The Word of God.
Our King wants men—volunteers; the service is
glorious, the victory is sure, the triumph eternal.
Who will follow? "Pray ye the Lord of the harvest, that he will send laborers into his harvest."

www.ingramcontent.com/pod-product-compliance
Lightning Source LLC
Chambersburg PA
CBHW022203020726
47496CB00008B/2859